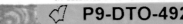

the different DRAGON

By Jennifer Bryan

Illustrated by Danamarie Hosler

Two Lives Publishing

Published by

Two Lives Publishing
www.TwoLives.com

Copyright © 2006 by

Jennifer Bryan

Illustrations copyright © 2006 by

Danamarie Hosler

Book design by

Desiree Rappa

ISBN

978-0-9674468-6-8

LCCN: 2005903058

2 3 4 5 6 7 8 9 10

For Noah, the hero of this adventure

and for Claire, whose story comes next.

Special thanks to Edward Babbott and Elizabeth Conant;

their support made the publication

of this book possible.

To Shiloh, who waited very patiently to go out,

and modeled a wonderful dragon.

Noah was a not-so-little boy who was getting ready for bed.

He had taken a bath.

He had chosen a favorite pair of pajamas and put them on all by himself.

He had brushed
his teeth and only
needed a little bit
of help from one
of his mothers
with flossing.

Then he built and toppled some block towers with
        his younger sister, Claire, on her bedroom floor;
chased the cat, Zoe, out of the hall closet;
        lined up all his toy trucks by the stairs,
wrestled with his momma and Claire
        in his parents' room and then finally
crashed the neat row of trucks into
        a big messy pile.
        It was a loud crash.

"I think you
are ready for bed,"
said Go-Ma.

"I think
you are right,"
said Noah, with a big gr

And when he was snuggled into his
cozy, big boy bed in his own room,
he said to Go-Ma, "Let's tell a story."
"Okay," said Go-Ma. "Who should be in it?"
          "Me!" said Noah.
"Will anybody else in the family be in it?" Go-Ma asked.
Noah was a boy who had two mothers
(Momma and Go-Ma), a younger sister (Claire),
two cats (Zoe and Diva), a gerbil (Rex) and some fish
          (Jonah, Scoopy and Tiny) in his family.
"Nope, just me," Noah said. Then he added,
          "Maybe Diva."
"All right," said Go-Ma. "And where should you be?"
"Hmmm," thought Noah. "How about on a boat?"
"Okay," said Go-Ma.

10

"Once upon a time, there was a boy named
Noah who went sailing on the ocean in his
royal blue and snappy orange boat."

"Is the boat an ocean liner or a sailboat?" asked Noah.
"A long, steady sailboat with silver sails and colorful flags
brought back from adventures in faraway places."
"Is there a moon?" asked Noah.

"Yes," answered Go-Ma. "He sailed along under a moonlit sky that was full of stars. Even though the boy was good at counting, there were so many stars in this night sky that he couldn't possibly count them all. The boat was sturdy and the water was dark and cool."

there music?" wondered Noah.

deed. Noah's favorite cat, Diva, always sailed on the royal blue
snappy orange boat with him. On this night she sang a fancy
he tune, opera style.

'I love a grand feast of big fishes from the sea.
I love a wicked prowl chasing mice and lots of fowl.
But what I love most is to nap, nap, nap
nap in the sun.'"

"Noah and Diva had discovered that magical things happened to them when they sailed the high seas under a moonlit sky. And tonight felt especially magical. As they stood on the deck of the boat looking out into the night, Noah tasted the air with his tongue.

He rolled the air around in his mouth and thought it tasted like..."

"Peanuts!" said Noah.
"Peanuts." Go-Ma agreed and went on. "Peanuts and lemons. And the magical-tasting air made Noah hungry for a snack. He said to Diva, 'Let's sail to Dragon Cove and get some chocolate yogurt for me and some goldfish for you.' Diva thought this was an excellent idea, so Noah turned the boat in the direction of Dragon Cove."

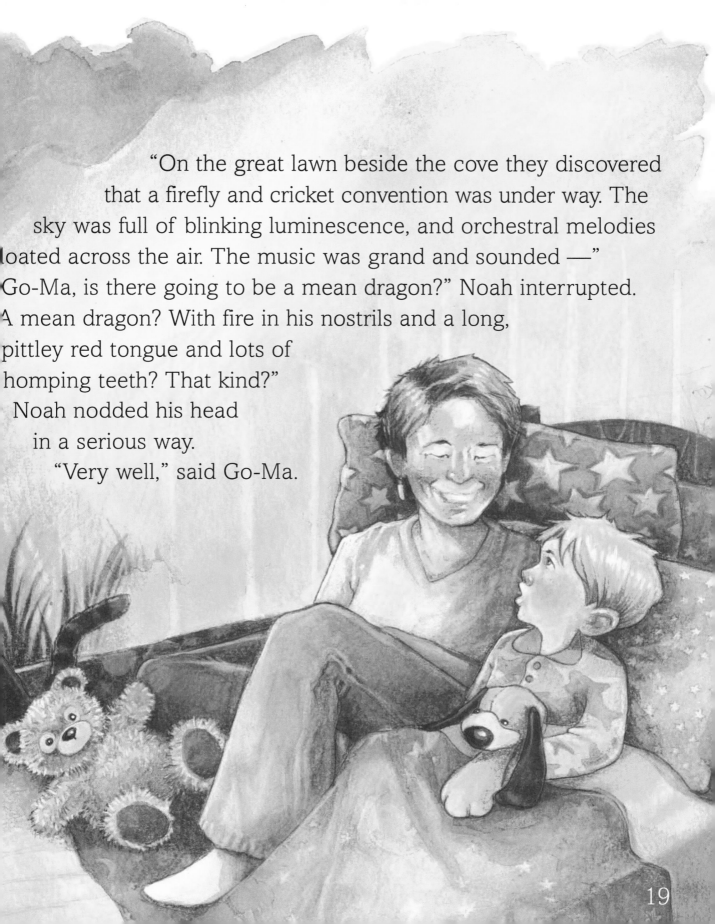

"On the great lawn beside the cove they discovered that a firefly and cricket convention was under way. The sky was full of blinking luminescence, and orchestral melodies floated across the air. The music was grand and sounded —"

"Go-Ma, is there going to be a mean dragon?" Noah interrupted.

"A mean dragon? With fire in his nostrils and a long, spittley red tongue and lots of chomping teeth? That kind?"

Noah nodded his head in a serious way.

"Very well," said Go-Ma.

"As Noah slipped the boat into the main dock in Dragon Cove, he felt a strangely warm gust of air brush the back of his neck. Diva meowed and then quickly skittled down below deck. Noah knew just what he would see when he turned around.

The meanest Dragon in all of Dragon County was lumbering down the hill, fire darting from each nostril and hot breath pouring from his teeth-filled mouth. The musical melodies abruptly ceased, and the crickets and fireflies scattered hither and yon. Noah stood on the deck of his boat and decided it was time to put on protective gear."

"A shield and goggles," Noah said.
"Right you are," said Go-Ma. "Noah went below deck. First he reassured Diva, who was hiding behind a pile of life-jackets, that all would be safe again soon. Then he donned his protective gear. When he went back up on deck, Noah saw that the dragon was beginning to ..."

21

"Cry," said Noah,
    quite certainly.
"Cry?" asked Go-Ma.
"Yes, because he's very upset."
"Why is he upset?"
"You tell," said Noah.

Go-Ma thought for a minute and then continued. "The dragon cried and cried. His sobs were so loud that they shook the trees and the ground and the hills and the very deck of Noah's sailboat. And the dragon's tears were as big as ..."

"Tennis balls," said Noah.

"Tennis balls, which splashed on the ground and began to make puddles all around the dragon. Noah, who had been prepared to protect himself from the dragon's fire, lowered his shield and pushed his goggles onto the top of his head. Then he spoke to the dragon. 'What's the matter?' he asked. 'I just can't do it,' the dragon wailed. His big nostrils were no longer darting fire; instead he had a runny nose, and truthfully, he could have used a very big handkerchief at that moment. 'It's no use.'

'What's no use?' Noah asked,
moving up to the bow of the boat
so he could get closer to the dragon,
who was now standing on the dock.
'I just can't be fierce anymore,'
the dragon said. 'I just can't.'
'Why not?' Noah asked.

'It's a lot of pressure to be fierce all the time. All that roaring and gnashing of teeth and snorting fire. It's a lot of work to scare people and be so mean. And nobody ever wants a dragon to be funny or sad or just regular. There's only one way for a dragon to be and that's that.' The dragon lay down, resting his head on his front legs, just the way Diva did when she was napping in the sun sometimes.

Noah put his shield down on the deck and spoke to the dragon kindly, but firmly. 'I am a smart boy and I know some things. I know that there are lots of different ways to be a dragon, and being fierce isn't the only way you have to be. You can be however you want. If you want to crush my sailboat and set it on fire and then eat me up, you can. Or we could play badminton and then have some ice cream instead.'

Noah did indeed sound very wise. The dragon listened carefully and thought about what Noah was saying. Then Noah added, 'And I have a lot of friends who feel the same as I do. They'd like a dragon who is different.'

With that, the dragon lifted his big head. He looked extremely relieved, even happy, and he dragged the scaly back of his claw across his runny nose.

'Can you teach me how to play badminton?' he asked.'

Noah said, 'Sure! Let me get the equipment.' So the very smart, not-so-little boy went below deck and retrieved two badminton racquets and a birdie.

Under the full moon he
taught the dragon how to play,
and they played for a
        long, long, long
time, until it was time for breakfast."

"And what did they have for breakfast?"
Noah asked with a yawn.

31

"Now that,"
    said his Go-Ma,
"is another story."

CPSIA information can be obtained
at www.ICGtesting.com
Printed in the USA
LVHW01n1327041018
592383LV00019B/239/P